# Rainbow

Rainbow
Published by Passage Point Publishing, Denver, CO

Publisher's Cataloging-in-Publication data

Title: Rainbow / Susan Lintonsmith ; illustrated by Tristram Drew.
Description: Denver, CO: Passage Point Publishing, 2021. | Summary: Ten-year-old Spencer and his annoying little brother, Justin, have discovered a magical world under the couch. They made it there and back safely once; can they do it again?
Identifiers: ISBN: 978-1-7368910-1-8
Subjects: LCSH Siblings--Juvenile fiction. | Fantasy fiction. | CYAC Siblings--Fiction. | BISAC JUVENILE FICTION / Fantasy & Magic | JUVENILE FICTION / Readers / Intermediate | JUVENILE FICTION / Family / Siblings
Classification: LCC PZ7.1.L5645 Rai | DDC [Fic]--dc23

ISBN: 978-1-7368910-1-8

Illustrations by Tristram Drew
Cover and Interior design by Laura Drew
Editing by Shelly Wilhelm

Quantity Purchases: Schools, companies, professional groups, clubs, and other organizations may qualify for special terms when ordering quantities of this title. For information, email susan@underthecouchbooks.com.

**PASSAGE
POINT
PUBLISHING**

# UNDER THE COUCH

BOOK
2

# Rainbow

## SUSAN LINTONSMITH

To my husband, Chris Linton-Smith,
who supported my dream of writing books
based on the stories I told our sons
when they were young.

# CONTENTS

Chapter One...................................................1

Chapter Two................................................. 9

Chapter Three.............................................. 17

Chapter Four................................................ 24

Chapter Five................................................ 31

Chapter Six..................................................38

Chapter Seven..............................................48

Chapter Eight............................................... 55

Chapter Nine................................................ 62

Chapter Ten..................................................70

Chapter Eleven.............................................79

Chapter Twelve.............................................87

# CHAPTER
# 1

"What do you know about Lori?" Spencer asked his mom as she filled the coffee pot with water. She was dressed in pants and a blazer for work, and her straight blond hair was pulled back.

"What do you mean?" she asked, turning to look at him.

"What do we know about her? About her

family? Do we know *anything*?"

"Of course. My mom knows a friend of her mother's. That's how I found Lori," his mom said.

"But what do we know about her?" Spencer pressed.

His mom gave him a strange look. "I saw her resume. I know she used to teach preschool and likes kids. My mom's friend knows her family," she said. "It's not like I hired a complete stranger off the street."

"I know," Spencer said, seeing that she was getting a little upset. He tried again to get his point across. "But we really don't know anything about who she is."

"I know she is always in a good mood, on time, and very reliable," his mother responded. "And she was available. Do you know how hard it was to find someone on this side of town for the summer? I tried for many weeks before the move."

Spencer knew she struggled to find someone to stay with them five days a week.

He had wished his grandma could watch them, but she couldn't do it all day, every day. She had health issues and got tired easily.

His mom looked at him with concern on her face. "Why do you ask? Is there something I need to know? Did something happen?"

Spencer poured cereal into his bowl and reached into the refrigerator for milk. He climbed back on the stool at the kitchen island and started to drown his cereal with milk.

"Hello?" his mother said. Spencer glanced up to see that she was still waiting for his response.

"No, nothing happened. It's just that she never talks about herself," Spencer said.

"Geez, you had me worried," his mother sighed. "If you want to get to know her better, just ask her questions. I'm sure she'll tell you what you think you need to know." She turned toward the garage as she heard the garage door. "That's her now." She looked up at the clock. "See? Always on time. Try talking to her. You're a quiet person, so maybe it's *you* who needs to talk more." His mom turned to leave the kitchen. "I'm going to see if Justin is awake so I can tell him goodbye."

Spencer watched his mother leave as Lori came through the garage door. He nodded to Lori as she entered the kitchen. She nodded back with a grin on her face. She set her big brown shoulder bag down on the kitchen counter. Spencer stared at it, wondering what was in there. He could tell by how the sides puffed out that she had a lot of stuff in it. He had seen her put some strange things in that bag in the last three weeks.

Lori had started being their nanny when they moved into their new house. His mom's new job was across town from their old house, so they had moved at the end of the school year. Spencer didn't want to tell his mom that he thought Lori was really odd and that she didn't answer his questions. He knew she must be hiding something. Spencer looked at her bag again, wishing he could look through it to find out more about her. But she always kept it zipped up and by her side. If he could see what was in her bag, he knew he could discover her secrets. He was determined to figure her out.

Spencer glanced up and saw Lori watching him stare at her bag. They locked eyes. Her dark brown eyes looked bigger through her thick glasses that were outlined with big black frames. Her face softened as she heard Justin enter the kitchen. Justin ran over to Lori and started chatting away. He had just woken up and was still in his superhero pajamas.

Spencer returned his attention to his cereal. He slowly tapped the pieces, dunking them under the milk. He liked his cereal better when the milk softened the marshmallows. He listened to Justin and shook his head. He didn't understand why his family liked Lori so much. Was he the only one who could see there was something strange about her? He glanced up to watch her face as she listened to Justin. Lori was the same age as his mother, but not as thin, and she had a round face and short black hair. He noticed her hair wasn't as spiky today, and he could see strands of gray hair poking through.

"Good morning," his mother said to Lori as she walked back into the kitchen. After they talked a few minutes, she turned to Justin. "Hey, make sure you read today." Spencer knew their mom was concerned that Justin struggled with reading. Her solution was to make both of them read every day.

"What?" Justin protested. "Like a book?"

"Yes, like a book. You don't have to read the whole thing, but at least try to read a chapter a day." She picked up the coffeepot to fill her mug.

"But it's summer!" Justin whined.

Spencer heard his mother sigh heavily as she placed her coffee down on the counter and turned back to face Justin. Her face softened. "Look, the more you read, the easier it will get. You have to be ready for second grade. Your teacher said to keep practicing over the summer, remember?"

Justin crossed his arms and crinkled his face. "I hate reading."

"You'll learn to love it when it gets easier. Maybe Ms. Lori can take you to the library today to pick out some books you'd like." Spencer smirked when he saw the look on Justin's face. He was clearly unhappy.

"We'll go to the library after lunch," Lori said, smiling and nodding.

Spencer heard a truck beeping next door. He turned to look out the window over the kitchen sink. A cement truck was backing into the dirt lot. He could see a few of the construction workers standing around talking. They were making progress on the new house. They had finished digging out the basement and were ready to pour the concrete.

"Spencer," his mother called, waving her hand in the air to get his attention. He turned away from the window to look at her. "I want you to read too."

He didn't say anything. He didn't feel like telling her that he read nearly every day. He had just finished his book on the phases of the moon and had started a book about the stars in the Milky Way. He was trying to memorize the star formations. He didn't mind reading if the book was about space.

"I have to get to work. I have a big meeting today," their mom said. She grabbed her lunch out of the refrigerator. "Dad will be home from his trip this afternoon, so you can tell us what you read about at dinner tonight, okay?"

Justin groaned. Spencer saw his mother smile as she gave him a big hug. She walked over and gave Spencer a quick hug, then grabbed her briefcase and headed out the door.

# CHAPTER
# 2

"You okay?" Lori asked.

Spencer was staring at his soggy cereal. Ever since his mother started her new job, she was always rushing and seemed a little more distant. And both of his parents were traveling more. They were busy all the time between the new house and their jobs. He looked up and saw that Lori was talking to him. "Yah," he responded.

"Look, your mom is just a little stressed. I think her new job is very demanding. Between the job and the move, she's tired. Why don't we do something nice for her today, like maybe make dinner?"

"Can we make mashed potatoes?" Justin asked.

"Of course," Lori said, patting down Justin's bedhead. His blond hair was sticking up on top.

Spencer thought she was different but liked that she was always in a good mood. He never felt cheery in the morning like Lori and Justin, especially since their move. He was still unhappy about leaving his old neighborhood and friends, and he was upset about having to go to a new school for fifth grade. He hated the idea of being the new kid and not having any friends. It wasn't easy for him to make new friends. And now, his parents were always busy, and he was stuck spending the summer with his annoying little brother and a strange nanny.

Spencer looked back at Lori as she laughed at something Justin had said. He watched the two of them. He sighed. Maybe his mother was right. Maybe he just needed to ask Lori more questions.

After breakfast, they headed to the park. Lori took them to the park every morning while the temperature was still relatively cool. The boys knew she didn't like the afternoon heat. Sometimes they drove to a new park, but typically, they walked to the park by their house. Lori liked that there were a lot of big trees between their new neighborhood and the park. She also liked to take her shoes off and sit on the grass under the shade of a tree to watch them play.

Spencer threw the baseball around with Justin. He was hoping he'd see someone his age who would want to play with them, but no luck. There were only young kids playing on the playground. They played for a few hours and then started to walk back to their house.

Lori walked slowly on the dirt path. She loved looking at the tall pine trees that were on both sides of the path. She took her time and looked around on the ground. They walked too slowly, so Spencer walked ahead of them. He could hear her reciting the names of the different trees and flowers. Justin walked next to her, asking questions and chatting away.

"Hold up, Spencer," Lori called. He stopped and looked back. Lori bent down to get something behind a tree. Spencer walked back toward her and saw her grab a clump of yellow dandelions. After she had picked a few handfuls, she looked around for more. When she had collected a bunch, she separated the flowers from the leaves and put them in different containers in her brown shoulder bag.

Spencer wondered what she was going to do with weeds. He knew his dad hated getting dandelions in their yard and sometimes used weedkiller on them. *But Lori collects them? This is probably part of her secret.* Spencer decided he was going to make a list of all the strange things she did. He knew he had to be careful, so she didn't figure out what he was doing. But he was determined to figure out what she was up to. He remembered what his mom had said and decided to start asking his questions.

"Where did you grow up, Ms. Lori?" he asked as they started walking again. He thought she might be more willing to talk as they walked.

"Oh, different parts of Colorado," she answered, looking around the tree trunks.

"Around here?" Spencer asked. She seemed to know all the parks in the area.

"Yes, here and a few other places," she answered.

Spencer was about to ask her about the other places, but she interrupted him.

"Look Justin, baby bunnies!" Justin ran over to where she was pointing. The two of them cooed over the bunnies. Spencer knew she was causing a distraction so she wouldn't have to answer his questions. She always found something else to focus on to avoid answering him.

After lunch, Lori took them to the library. Spencer had told Justin to hurry so they could get home in time for Lori's TV show. He wanted to try and go under the couch while she watched her afternoon program. That's when they had gone on their first adventure the previous week. He and Justin had tried to go several times over the weekend while their parents were busy, but it didn't work. They couldn't get through. Spencer thought about it all weekend. *Do we have to go on a certain day or maybe a certain time of day? Or is it possible that our first trip under the couch was a one-time fluke?*

When they got home from the library, Spencer stood by the kitchen sink, watching the cement truck next door. He glanced up again at the kitchen clock. The big hand had only moved two minutes since the last time he looked. Time was moving too slowly. He heard Justin behind him.

"Is it almost time to go?" Justin whispered.

"Ten minutes until her show starts," Spencer whispered back. Justin smiled his crooked grin. Spencer knew Justin was excited about going back under the couch. It was all he talked about since their first trip.

"I hope we get through today," Justin said softly. Spencer nodded. He did too. He had to go back to find what he left behind on the first trip. He was disappointed that they weren't able to get through over the weekend. He and Justin talked about it and decided to try again while Lori was there. But so far that week, they hadn't had a chance to try because she was always with them. The only time she took a break from them was to occasionally watch her show. That was her time to relax, and it was the time it had worked before. Spencer wanted to make sure they tried at the exact same time today.

He continued watching the cement truck as Lori brushed past him to make her hot tea. Spencer glanced over to watch her rifle through her shoulder bag. She pulled out a strange-looking tea bag. After boiling the water and making her tea, she grabbed her shoulder bag and headed into the family room. She dropped her bag next to her chair and turned on the TV. Spencer eyed the bag. He noticed that once again, she had taken it with her. It was almost as if she *knew* he wanted to look through it.

# CHAPTER
# 3

"Spencer, do you want to watch this show with me?" Lori called over her shoulder. "It's an interesting topic today that I think you might like."

"What's it about?" Spencer asked.

"Space aliens. They are interviewing people who claim to have seen them. They also are talking to a pilot who claims he has seen several spaceships while flying over New Mexico and the Northwest coast."

Spencer felt torn. He loved anything about space and wanted to know more about aliens. But he really wanted to try to go under the couch. He looked over at Justin and saw him shaking his head no.

"No thanks. I'll read with Justin while you watch it," Spencer responded.

Lori looked at Spencer strangely. "You will?" she asked, surprised.

"What? No!" Justin yelled. Spencer winked at Justin to let him know to play along. He didn't want Lori to get suspicious. She had a way of knowing things.

"Come on, Justin, Mom said you need to read every day," Spencer said. Justin understood what he was doing and whined a little more to make it look real. He then turned and tried to wink back at Spencer but ended up closing both of his eyes.

"Well, okay. I'm here if you guys change your mind or if you need anything," Lori said.

As they went into the living room, Spencer could feel the fluttering in his stomach. He was nervous about going back under the couch. The first trip had been so stressful, and he had worried the entire time about how they were going to get back home. He hadn't planned to go again, but that changed when he realized he had left his black-braided chain and pendant behind. It was a special gift from his grandma for his tenth birthday. She had been so excited to give it to him. She knew he loved space and had it custom-made for him with a crescent moon and stars on one side of the pendant and the infinity sign on the other. Spencer remembered having it last in the square room. He had been so anxious and remembered touching it a lot. For some reason, the pendant helped him feel less anxious. Now he had to go back to the square room to find it.

Spencer looked at the oversized cream-colored couch that his dad bought at an antique store in the mountains. It didn't look around 200 years old because the fabric was newer. Their dad liked that it was massive and well-built. Justin liked to hide under it because it was tall with a skirt that touched the floor. Spencer hadn't paid much attention to the couch until nearly a week ago. Now, he knew there was something special about it.

"I'll go first," Justin said as he got down on the floor to lift the couch skirt. He crawled under, talking the entire time. "I hope it works. I'll try to do exactly what I did the first time."

Spencer got down on his stomach and poked his head under the couch skirt so he could watch Justin disappear. He was eager to figure out how it happened. He didn't understand how they could fall under the couch. Justin didn't care *how* it happened — he just wanted to go again. Spencer watched as Justin pressed his entire body against the wall at the back of the couch.

"I can't wait to go on the slide again!" Justin yelled.

"Wait, don't go yet. I can't see very well," Spencer whispered as he started to back out.

"I want to grab a flashlight so I can watch what happens." He didn't hear a response. "Justin? Did you hear me?" Spencer stuck his head back under the couch but only saw the wall. Justin was already gone. *It worked!*

While he was happy that Justin made it through, Spencer was disappointed that he didn't get to see him disappear. He decided to skip getting the flashlight and follow his brother. He didn't want to leave Justin alone in the dark hallway.

As he crawled under the couch, Spencer could feel the pangs growing in his stomach. He felt nervous because he didn't know what kind of danger they could face. They made it safely back the last time, but he didn't know if it would be the same this time. He was starting to second guess whether he really wanted to go, but Justin had already gone so there was no turning back.

Spencer pressed himself parallel to the wall and waited. Nothing happened. He pressed a little closer. Nothing. He rolled over to face the wall and put his hand against it. *Why isn't it working for me?* Spencer figured it had to be the right time of day since it had worked for Justin. His heart started pounding faster as he worried about what would happen to Justin if he couldn't get through. Would Justin be stuck there? Spencer took several deep breaths to relax. Then he wondered if he was supposed to face the other way. He started to flip over.

The next thing Spencer knew, he felt like he was falling over a ledge. His body jerked, and his stomach lurched as he fell. Then he felt the cool, smooth steel surface under him. This time, he knew what to expect. He wasn't going to go down the slide headfirst like before. On his first ride, he had flown off the slide and landed on the ground on his stomach. This time, he planned to land on his feet.

Spencer was going so fast that it was hard for him to turn around. Finally, he got his feet in front of him. Then the speed forced him to lie back as he sped around the wide circles. He slid faster as the circles got tighter. He tried to drag the heels of his white sneakers to slow down, but it didn't work. The surface was too slick. After countless turns, he flew off the bottom of the slide. He fought to get his feet under him. He cheered as he landed on his feet . . . until the motion propelled him forward.

# CHAPTER 4

Spencer tried to break his fall with his hands but felt his face smack into the padding on the floor. He could hear loud laughter echoing through the dark hallway as he lay on the mat. The strong rubber scent from the floor filled his sore nose. He cursed under his breath. He thought for sure he would land on his feet. He lifted his head and looked over at Justin, who was bent over, holding his stomach as he laughed.

"You should have seen yourself!" Justin roared. "You did a total face plant! That was hilarious!" Justin could barely catch his breath he was laughing so hard.

Spencer glared at him and tried to sit up. "Okay, next time, I go first. Then I can watch *you* land on your face!"

"I landed on my feet," Justin told him, wiping his eyes, and trying to stop laughing. "Both times."

"Right," Spencer grumbled as he slowly picked himself up from the mat. He brushed off his white T-shirt and adjusted his gray gym shorts. He stepped off the soft padding and onto the matted floor. He rubbed his stinging nose and checked to make sure it wasn't bleeding. He was glad the ground in front of the slide was well-padded.

Spencer looked around, blinking his eyes in the dark. Now he wished he had grabbed the flashlight and made Justin wait. At least his annoying brother had stopped laughing. Spencer looked down the hallway. He wondered if the place would be less creepy with more light. There had to be a way to make the lights brighter. He hadn't seen any light switches on the last trip, but he hadn't looked everywhere since he had been too busy trying to get back up the slide.

Spencer looked around on both sides of the hall. He not only didn't see any light switches, but he also didn't see any fixtures. He glanced up at the high ceiling. It was solid, like the walls, with no lights. The only light he could see seemed to be coming from *inside* the strange walls.

"Look for lights or switches down there," he called to Justin, who was skipping up and down the hallway, chattering about his ride down the slide.

As Justin looked, Spencer stood in the middle of the floor and stared at the wall. From the shiny surface, he could see the reflection of his white shirt and light brown hair. Around his reflection were flickers of light. He walked to the wall and ran his fingertips across it. The surface was cool and smooth like the slide. But it was more translucent than steel since light was passing through. He looked into the wall but couldn't tell the source of the light. He thought it looked like the flames from candles. *But how can there be candles in a wall?* He wondered as he knocked on the surface. It was solid, but he wasn't sure if it was glass, steel, or another material.

He knocked again to see if he could tell. Then something inside the wall returned the knock. Spencer jumped back in fright and stared at the wall. It was quick, but he thought he saw another reflection . . . *in* the wall. Chills went through his body. He knew it wasn't his reflection. And he knew it wasn't Justin. He could hear him at the other end of the hall talking. Spencer stepped forward and leaned his face against the wall to get a closer look. He was trying to see if there was a room on the other side. Then he saw a large green eye looking back at him! He yelped and jumped back and nearly fell as his legs got tangled up. He caught his balance and stood up. He was frozen. His heart was racing, and his body was shaking. He looked back at the wall, but this time didn't see the green eye. He tried to calm down, taking deep breaths. Did he really see a reflection and an eyeball inside the wall? He jumped again when he heard another knock behind him.

He turned around quickly, fists in a fighting position, ready to deal with whatever was behind him. Justin was standing at the opposite wall. He had his hand in a fist and was getting ready to knock again.

"Why are we knocking?" Justin asked.

Spencer growled at him, "*I* was knocking because I'm trying to figure out these walls. I don't know why you're knocking."

"I was just copying you," Justin innocently explained. "Why did you scream?"

"I didn't scream," Spencer shot back.

"Yes you did. You sounded like this." Justin

screamed to show Spencer what he sounded like. The noise echoed through the hall.

"I didn't sound like that!" Spencer shouted. He wondered if he should tell Justin what he had seen in the wall. His brother was only seven years old, and Spencer didn't want to scare him. Plus, Spencer wasn't sure exactly what he saw. He decided not to tell Justin. Not yet. "Did you see any light switches down there?"

"No, nothing. Can we go through the door now?" Justin asked.

"Okay," Spencer said reluctantly.

Justin skipped happily back down the hallway. Spencer didn't understand how his brother wasn't bothered by the dark hallway and the creepy walls.

Spencer followed behind him, watching the wall out of the corners of his eyes as he walked. On his left, he could see the lights in the wall sway as he passed by, almost like flames dancing with the breeze of his movement. Or was it from the movement of someone *inside* the wall? Spencer got chills again. "This place is so creepy," he mumbled as he joined Justin at the end of the hallway. "Ready?" Spencer asked.

This time, they knew how to open the door. They had learned from their first trip that they needed to work together in the under-the-couch world. Justin reached out and placed his left hand on the big metal latch. Spencer put his hand beside it. They gripped the handle, and the black door slowly swung toward them. It opened a few feet to allow them through. Spencer saw moonlight streaming through the door. He was happy to step into the lighter and warmer circular room. As Spencer followed Justin into the room, he heard the giant door close tightly behind them. Spencer turned and looked at it.

"Justin, touch the handle with me. I just want to see if it opens again." They touched the big metal handle at the same time. The door did not move. It remained solidly shut.

# CHAPTER
# 5

Spencer stared at the shut door. He didn't understand why it had opened for them a second ago, but not now. Was the door waiting for them to do something first? Spencer knew the same thing happened last time. The door wouldn't open until *after* their adventure. He didn't understand how the door knew when to open for them.

Spencer shook his head as he turned to take in the big circular room. Again, the sight of the room took his breath away. He was excited to see the amazing domed ceiling that looked like a real night sky. He looked over at the blue marble in the center of the room. He wanted to run over to see it, but first wanted to find his chain and pendant. He had to get back into the square room since that was the place he last remembered having it. He recalled that he was hiding from Justin and got trapped. He was panicking and had touched the pendant to calm down. He knew the chain had to be in that room. Now he had to find the square door to get back there.

Spencer looked over at the wall and frowned. He didn't see it. He walked around the entire room, but still couldn't find it.

"Justin, stop running around and help me find the square door!" Spencer yelled over to his brother as he walked back to the spot on the wall where he thought it was. "You can play once we get my pendant back." He remembered the door being about halfway around the room from the entrance, but it seemed like a different door was now in that spot. Justin came up behind him.

"Wasn't the door around here?" Spencer asked, motioning to the wall.

"I think so," Justin said, looking around. "But I don't see it."

"It has to be here!" Spencer said, feeling panicked. "We have to find it."

Justin shook his head. "I don't see it."

Spencer pointed to the left. "You go around the room that way, and I'll go this way. Look carefully!" Justin took off to the left, and Spencer went right. They met on the other side of the room.

"Still didn't see it," Justin said.

"That's not possible! Okay, keep going around. Maybe one of us missed it." The boys continued walking around the circular room until they met back at the point where they had started.

"Nope, not there." Justin shrugged his shoulders.

"How could this be happening?" Spencer asked sadly. "I can't believe the square door is gone. Now I have to tell Grandma I lost the pendant." He had been convinced that he'd find his chain and pendant if they could get back to this room. Now he had to accept that the square door and his necklace were gone for good.

Justin stood next to him. "I'm sorry about your pendant," he said. Then, as if he couldn't hold it in any longer, he blurted out, "Since we're here, can we go on another adventure? Please?"

Spencer had told Justin that once he got his pendant back, they could discuss it. He could see how excited Justin was to go and he was right, they were already there. But Spencer was nervous about going through another door. They had no way of knowing what would be on the other side. Spencer looked back at the hallway door. He knew in his gut it wasn't going to open for them. Not yet. It was as if the door was on Justin's side and wanted them to go on an adventure.

Spencer sighed. "Okay, I guess we can."

Justin cheered. "I get to pick the door since you chose the boring square one last time."

Spencer thought about that for a minute. "Okay, but you can't pick a big or scary-looking door. And we take turns. I get to pick next time."

"Next time?" Justin asked with a big smile on his face.

"I mean *if* we come back again. Let's see how today goes."

Justin ran over to the wall, talking excitedly about picking the best door. Upset about not finding his pendant, Spencer looked up at the dome-shaped ceiling. He gazed at the sparkling stars and four moons that were lighting the circular room. This was the most amazing ceiling — better than at the planetarium. Except this ceiling had four moons. He crinkled his brow as he studied the moons. They were no longer perfect circles. Nearly a week ago, they were full moons, but today they were smaller.

"They're gibbous moons! Waning gibbous moons!" Spencer knew that term from the book he had just finished.

"Huh?" Justin asked from across the room.

"Look at the moons. They are all about three-quarters of a circle, which is a gibbous moon. The moons had been full but now are waning, which means getting smaller." He scratched his head, trying to think. *How is that possible? Of course, this isn't a real sky, especially with four moons. But how can moons change shapes on a ceiling?*

Everything looked so real to him. The ceiling looked like it went on forever. Spencer studied the bright, sparkling stars. He had started his book on the stars in the Milky Way and memorized a few of the easier formations. He wanted to see if he could find them on this ceiling. First, he looked for the Big Dipper, which he knew was part of the Ursa Major constellation. He couldn't find it. He looked for the Little Dipper, which he had recently learned was part of Ursa Minor. He frowned when he couldn't find that either. He continued looking for Orion, Taurus, and Gemini. He didn't find any of the constellations that can be seen from earth. *Where are we?*

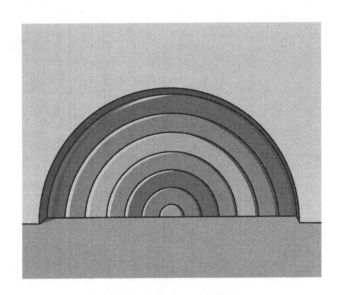

# CHAPTER
# 6

"Spencer!" Justin shouted as he grabbed his brother's arm.

"Ouch! Don't do that!" Spencer said, trying to smack him back.

"I was talking to you!" Justin said.

Spencer looked at his brother's face. He didn't understand why Justin got so frustrated with him. "I was busy looking. I didn't hear you," Spencer said, rubbing his arm.

"I know! You were lost in the ceiling. Dad is right — your head is in space!"

Spencer started to chase his brother, but Justin was fast and got away quickly. Spencer stopped racing after him and looked back up at the ceiling, still angry. He hated when Justin said that. His head wasn't in space. There was nothing strange about admiring a ceiling filled with so many stars and moons. He thought it was such a peculiar ceiling. Maybe Justin didn't understand.

"I don't get why there are four moons. And how did they change from full moons last week to gibbous moons today? And look at the stars. I don't recognize any of the formations," Spencer said out loud, trying to explain his thoughts.

"Who cares!" Justin replied, standing a safe distance away. "It's a ceiling. Can we please go on our adventure now?"

Spencer looked over at the blue marble glowing in the middle of the room. He really wanted to spend time looking at it. "Can I just look at the marble for a minute?"

"Can't you do that when we get back?" Justin pleaded. "I've already waited a long time for you."

Spencer knew his brother was eager to get going. "Okay," he sighed. "I'll look at the marble after our adventure."

"I found a great door!" Justin said, running to the wall and pointing. "Do you like it?"

Spencer walked over to see Justin's choice. The door was a semi-circle with the straight part flat to the floor. The highest point of the circular section was about nine feet tall. He could see why Justin picked this door. It had several different colors layered on top of each other, like a rainbow. Spencer looked at his brother's colorful striped shirt. Justin liked color.

"You okay with this door? I didn't pick a door that was big or scary."

"Yes," Spencer replied. He had to admit that he liked the door. "But I don't see a door handle. I'm not sure how we open it."

Justin looked back at the door. "What should we do?"

"Let's try a few spots and see if that works." Spencer placed his hand on the colorful door. Justin did the same. Nothing happened.

"Maybe we should touch the same place?" Justin asked. They tried a few places. The door shook a little but didn't open.

"Touch it here — in the middle," Spencer said, pointing at what he thought was the center. Spencer felt the butterflies in his stomach, feeling anxious about what would be on the other side of the door. He looked over and saw Justin grinning. His little brother was excited and didn't worry about running into danger. The boys placed their left palms flat in the middle of the arc-shaped door. They watched as the arc lifted up like a garage door. Justin giggled as they walked through the opening. Once they were on the other side of the door, it closed back to the ground.

Spencer looked around. They were standing in a meadow of tall green grass and purple and yellow wildflowers. In the distance, he saw rolling hills as well as patches of beautiful pink and white flowering dogwood trees.

"My shoes are wet," Justin announced. Spencer looked down at his brother's white slip-on shoes that weren't so white. Their mother said that Justin could get dirty within minutes of waking up. Justin liked shoes that didn't have shoelaces. He couldn't tie his shoes well, so his laces usually dragged on the ground. Spencer could feel water seeping into his own white sneakers.

"It just rained," Spencer said, noticing the droplets hanging on to the tall grass. He breathed deeply. He loved the smell of rain. It was humid and warm here — warmer than the circular room. He looked up and saw the sun peeking out from behind the clouds. "Looks like the rain moved to the other side of the field."

"Look!" Justin shouted, pointing behind them. Spencer turned and saw that the door they had come through was gone.

"Where did the door go? What's with all

the doors disappearing?" Spencer asked.

"No, not that. Look over there!" Justin pointed across the meadow. "A ginormous rainbow!" Spencer looked and saw the biggest rainbow he had ever seen. It reached from one end of the sky to the other. Each band of color was wide and vibrant as if competing to out-sparkle its neighbor.

Justin stretched his left arm up high in the sky, pointing at the rainbow. He started naming off the colors starting at the top: "Red, orange, yellow, green, blue . . . " He hesitated, not sure what to call the last two colors. He finally decided. "Purples."

"Indigo and violet," Spencer told him.

Justin's brow furrowed. "You made that up."

"No, I didn't. The last two colors are indigo and violet. ROY-G-BIV."

"ROY-G what?"

"R-O-Y-G-B-I-V," Spencer spelled out. "It's the acronym for the colors of a rainbow."

"I don't know what an *anocrim* is."

"*Acronym.* Yes, you do, it's an abbreviation from the first letters of each word. Like ASAP stands for as soon as possible."

"Oh. Well, I don't know what ROY-G-whatever is," Justin said.

"ROY-G-BIV is an acronym for the colors of the rainbow — red, orange, yellow, green, blue, indigo, and violet. Don't you remember Dad telling us that?" Spencer asked.

"Nope," Justin said, shaking his head and still gazing in the sky. "I've never seen such a big rainbow."

Spencer agreed. He had seen many rainbows caused by afternoon rains, but never one like this.

"Let's go touch it," Justin suggested, looking like he was getting ready to run.

"It's farther away than you think. Besides, it's just water vapor. It would probably feel like running through a mist."

"If it's just water, then how does it get all those colors?" Justin asked.

Spencer tried to remember how his dad

had explained it to him. "See how the sun is behind us and the rainbow is in the other part of the sky where it's raining?"

Justin looked from the sun to the rainbow and nodded.

"It has something to do with the sun's rays going through the water droplets. When the rays hit the water, they bend. What we see are the colors." Spencer wasn't sure he had it exactly right but figured Justin didn't know the difference. He continued to tell Justin what he remembered their dad saying. "Did you know that when the sun is higher in the sky, like today, the rainbow looks lower to the ground?" He wasn't sure if Justin was listening. His younger brother was busy gazing at the rainbow.

# CHAPTER
## 7

"I want to touch it. In fact, I want to go *through* it!" Justin said. He stretched out his arms dramatically and shouted, "I *wish* we could go through the giant rainbow!" His voice echoed through the peaceful meadow. He laughed as he saw a group of birds fly away, frightened by his loud voice. Spencer shook his head and started explaining again that you can't touch a rainbow. Before he could get more than a few words out, he felt a strong wind behind them. It came out of nowhere and was so strong that Spencer, even at nearly five feet tall and seventy pounds, was having trouble staying on the ground. Justin was only four feet tall and under fifty pounds and was immediately lifted off the ground. Spencer grabbed his colorful shirt with one hand and his right wrist with his other hand. He tried to pull him down to the ground. Justin's legs lifted in the air, and he turned upside-down. His shirt was falling over his face.

"Grab my hand!" Spencer yelled. The wind was getting stronger.

"Let go!" Justin yelled through his shirt. "You're hurting my wrist."

"No!" Spencer held on tighter, not wanting his brother to be carried away. *I can't let the wind take him! Where did this wind come from?* Spencer wondered, pulling Justin down with all his strength.

"Spencer, let go!" Justin yelled. Spencer gripped Justin's wrist harder and pulled.

"Hang on!"

"It's okay," Justin hollered through his shirt and the wind. "Let go — I want to fly!"

Spencer had no choice. The wind was too strong, and he was having a hard time staying on the ground. The wind jerked Justin out of his grasp. Horrified, he watched as the wind took Justin away.

"JUSTIN!" Spencer shouted as he watched his brother fly about twenty feet in the air and shoot across the open field. Spencer thought he was going to be sick. He knew if anything happened to Justin, his parents would never forgive him! He knew they shouldn't have gone back under the couch. He knew it was too dangerous.

Spencer yelled as loud as he could, but it was useless. He could barely see Justin. The wind had carried him away. He should have held on tighter. He shouldn't have let go. He was panicking and afraid that Justin was going to get hurt . . . or worse!

Spencer bent down and grabbed the wet tall grass around him, determined to stay on the ground. But he was no match for the wind. It built below him and lifted him up off the ground. He struggled with all his might. He lifted about three feet in the air. He flailed his arms around, fighting to get back on the ground. He landed on the wet grass and grabbed hold of the plants around him again. This time, the wind picked him up legs first. Spencer was upside down, hanging on to the grass. The wind was too strong, and it pulled him up into the air. Spencer fought and tried to flip around, hitting the ground on his side. The thick tall grass cushioned his fall. He continued to be pulled into the air, fight, and land back on the ground. Spencer realized that each time, he was going higher and hitting the ground harder. It was starting to hurt more when he landed on the ground.

As Spencer was pulled back into the air again, he heard a voice whispering close to his ear: "Let go." He whipped his head around to see who was talking to him. He knew it wasn't Justin's voice but didn't know who else it could be. He didn't see anyone.

"Relax . . . go with the flow," he heard the whisper in his ears.

"Who . . . who are you?" Spencer yelled with a shaky voice. He knew he couldn't stop struggling. He saw what had happened to Justin. He knew the wind would carry him far away.

"It's okay. Let go," came the whisper again. It was the same thing Justin had said to him. Still, he saw no one around. It was only him . . . fighting against the wind. *Is the wind talking to me?* He was tired from struggling and being bounced on the ground. He took the voice's advice and stopped fighting. He could feel the wind under him, taking him higher in the sky. It was hard, but the more he relaxed, the gentler the wind was with him. He flipped around for several minutes until he finally made his body relax. Once he did, he felt like he was floating in the air. He was still tense but was no longer bouncing on the ground. After several more minutes, the wind started to move him.

"No! Please!" Spencer cried. "Don't carry me off!"

"It's okay," the voice whispered again. "Go with the flow." He had no choice. He relaxed as the wind moved him across the field. Spencer watched as the earth moved quickly under him. He had no idea where the wind was taking him.

"Look," the voice said softly. Spencer looked around and spotted Justin. He saw with amazement that Justin was high over the meadow, flying around in circles.

"Thank you," Spencer said, relieved to see his brother. He had been afraid that Justin was hurt or lost, but Justin wasn't worried at all. Instead, he was hooting with delight. He waved excitedly at Spencer, with a huge smile on his face.

"Isn't this awesome?" Justin shouted to him. "Watch this!" Spencer watched as Justin dove up and down in a controlled wavy pattern. Then he flew higher in the air and did several loops. Not once did he come close to falling on the ground.

When he saw how much fun Justin was having, Spencer relaxed even more. He tried to copy some of Justin's stunts. It was difficult at first, but the more he relaxed, the easier it became. The wind did most of the work. He only had to move his body in the direction he wanted to go, and the wind pushed him along. He found that once he no longer struggled, he didn't have to worry about being dropped to the ground. He started to trust that the wind wouldn't hurt him. Soon, he was able to do the tricks that Justin was doing and started making up new ones for Justin to follow.

"Time to go. Lie flat," the wind whispered. Spencer watched as Justin got into a superhero position, with his stomach toward the ground and his legs and arms outstretched. Spencer copied him, and the wind pushed them through the air.

# CHAPTER
# 8

Spencer could hear Justin laughing. He knew his brother was loving this. He was too. He couldn't remember being this happy. He had always wanted to fly. He had dreams about flying, where he'd flap his arms and lift off the ground. But in his dreams, when he looked down, he realized people on the ground were watching him . . . and he was wearing only his underwear. He was always so happy to wake up from those dreams. Now he was really flying, and it wasn't a dream! He looked down to see that he still was wearing his white shirt and gray shorts, and he laughed.

As they flew with the wind, Spencer watched the rolling hills of the field underneath. They flew high above the patch of dogwood trees that were in full bloom as if spring had just arrived. The pink and white blooms against the tall green grass filled with purple and yellow wildflowers were an explosion of color to his eyes. Spencer was grateful to the wind for this rare treat. He wondered why he had struggled so hard against it.

"All you had to do was let go," the wind softly whispered.

"We're almost at the rainbow!" Justin shouted excitedly. Spencer saw the rainbow in front of them. He was awed by its size and brilliant colors. The wind slowed, but they stayed high in the air moving toward the rainbow. Justin stretched his fingers out in front of him, trying to touch the brilliant colors that stretched in an arc through the sky.

"It's just water," Spencer said out loud, but more to himself.

Suddenly, the wind shot them straight up in the sky to the very top of the rainbow. Spencer saw red mist as the wind pushed them directly into it. He felt liquid splashing him, like he was going through a small waterfall on a water ride at the amusement park. He could feel the wet drops on his bare arms and face. He closed his eyes as he was pushed through the red spray to the other side. The splashing stopped and he blinked his eyes as he rubbed the red liquid off his face. He felt the wind slowly turning him around. Spencer looked at the shimmering red arc they had just passed through. He looked at his clothes. His white T-shirt was completely splattered in red as if it had been spray-painted. He looked over and saw that his brother was covered in red liquid too. His colorful shirt was now a bright red.

Justin waved to Spencer with one hand and licked red liquid off his other hand.

"Tastes like cherry!" Justin yelled over. Even Justin's teeth were red from the rainbow.

Spencer laughed and licked his lips. Justin was right. It tasted like sweet cherry. He licked the back of his hand. It was like liquid candy.

After a short rest, the wind started to pick up again. Spencer got excited, anticipating going through again. This time, the wind wasn't as gentle as it tossed them back toward the brilliant colors. It was as if they were on a rubber band being shot through the air and into the rainbow. They were under the red layer heading directly for the orange. Spencer could hear Justin roar with laughter. As they approached, Justin opened his mouth and stuck out his tongue. Spencer copied him to catch orange liquid in his mouth. They were in the orange section for about ten seconds, being smacked in the face with orange droplets. The wind slowed down as they exited the rainbow, back on the side where they started off. They were stopped in midair, as if caught in a net. They rested for a minute, and then the wind slowly turned them around. They trusted the wind to keep them in the air.

Now the boys were completely soaked. Spencer looked over at Justin. He was covered in a reddish-orange liquid.

"Yum, orange!" Justin shouted over, licking his arms and hands as they rested. Spencer licked the liquid off his hands too. He liked the orange even more than the red cherry. Suddenly, the wind picked up and shot them back at the rainbow. This time, they were heading into the yellow section, below the orange. Spencer braced for getting smacked with what he anticipated would be a tart lemon flavor. He was pleasantly surprised when he licked his lips, and the flavor was sweet pineapple.

Once through the yellow part of the rainbow, they were given another quick break. The wind blew straight up from the ground, keeping them safely in the air as they wiped their faces and tried to open their eyes. This was better than any ride at an amusement park. Now Spencer was fully relaxed and enjoying himself. He looked at his shirt. It looked mostly orange from the combination of reds, oranges, and yellows. Before he had time to get the sweet pineapple off his face and hands, the wind flung them back toward the rainbow. This time, they went directly through the green section. Spencer wasn't sure what flavor to expect. *Will it be a tart lime?* He opened his mouth wide and closed his eyes when the spray hit him.

"Sour apple!" he heard Justin shout. Spencer loved sour green apple. It was delicious but a big contrast to the sweet cherry, orange, and pineapple flavors. The green made his eyes sting and his mouth pucker.

When they got to the other side, Justin was laughing and pointing at him. "You got slimed!"

Spencer looked over at Justin and joined his laughter. His brother's messy hair was completely green. It looked like someone had thrown a can of green paint at him. "You look like you're from outer space!"

Next, the wind threw them through the blue section, which tasted like blueberry. The indigo was less sweet than the blueberry. It tasted like red and black raspberries. They were lower to the ground now, ready to go through the violet color at the bottom of the rainbow. The wind was careful not to throw them as hard. Spencer and Justin opened their mouths wide to enjoy the spray of delicious grape before the wind gently placed them back on the ground.

"That was the best ever!" Justin jumped up and down with excitement. He looked over at Spencer and laughed. "You look so funny!"

"You do too!" The whites of Justin's eyes stood out from all the colors on his face and in his hair. Spencer looked down and saw that his white shirt and white sneakers were bluish-purple. He joined Justin in licking the colors off his hands and arms.

# CHAPTER 9

"That was awesome!" Justin said, grinning from ear to ear.

The boys sat on the wet ground and rested. They were tired from being tossed around in the air. They watched as the clouds moved on and the rainbow slowly disappeared.

"Who would have thought you could actually go *through* a rainbow. And taste it too. I mean, a rainbow is actually light and water droplets," Spencer said, shaking his head in disbelief.

"It was a giant magic rainbow. This whole place is magical," Justin said, moving his arms around.

"Giant magic rainbow," Spencer repeated. He was quiet for a few minutes, deep in thought, wondering how all this happened. "Hey, what exactly did you yell out before the wind picked you up?"

"I wanted to touch the rainbow," Justin said, scrunching up his face in thought. "I yelled that I wished we could go through it."

"You *wished* it!" Spencer exclaimed.

Justin nodded his head, looking eagerly at his brother.

"Don't you see? You made a big wish on the giant rainbow, and it came true!"

"Like making a wish on a shooting star?" Justin asked, excited that he was the one who made all of this happen.

"Yes." Spencer couldn't believe that

Justin's crazy wish had come true. The boys sat and looked at each other, taking it all in. They still couldn't get over how the other one looked, drenched in the rainbow colors.

"I should have wished for a motorcycle too," Justin said as he stood up and looked around to see if there were any more rainbows in the sky.

"No Justin, it was the perfect wish. That was amazing." Spencer stood up as well, noticing that grass and mud were sticking to him. The liquid candy from the rainbow had dried, leaving him sticky all over. "I don't know how we're going to explain to Lori how our clothes got like this," he said, looking down at his blue-stained shirt. "And I'm a little bummed about ruining my new white sneakers." Now that the fun was over, Spencer started worrying. "I'm not sure how we're going to get back. The door was way over there," he said, pointing across the field. "Maybe we should start walking."

"Maybe the wind can take us back," Justin suggested.

"I wish it would. I wish it would help us get clean too. I'm a sticky mess," Spencer said, not really believing that it was possible.

The boys felt the wind picking up again. Like before, it circled around them and lifted them up. This time, Spencer didn't resist. He had thought he was finished flying and was excited to be back in the air. He could hear Justin laughing with excitement. They stuck their arms straight out to fly like superheroes. The wind carried them across the fields, past the pink and white flowering dogwood trees, to a clear lake that was tucked away behind a steep hill.

It suddenly stopped, dropping the boys into a big lake in front of a waterfall. Spencer loved falling into the cool water. It felt so good after being hot and sticky. He sank quickly to the bottom and felt the pain in his ears. The spot where the wind dropped them was a little deeper than the pool near their house. Spencer pushed hard on the bottom to get back up to the surface.

When he got his head above the water, he took a big breath of air and treaded water. He was struggling to stay above water while he looked around for Justin. He knew his brother wasn't a strong swimmer. He didn't see him. Panicked, he stuck his head under the water to look. The water was clear, and he could see Justin closer to the waterfall. His little brother was still underwater, struggling to get to the surface. Spencer swam over and dove under him. He pushed Justin away from the waterfall and up toward the surface. He pushed with all his strength. He continued swimming and pushing until Justin got his head above the surface of the water. Then Spencer struggled to get his own head above water to get another breath of air.

As soon as his head broke the surface of the water, Spencer yelled, "Help! Please, help me!" before going back under the water to help his brother.

Spencer tried to swim and pull Justin with him toward the shore. But he was tired and kept getting dragged under the water. He let go of Justin to get more air. He looked around and saw Justin below the surface. He yelled again for help and saw a big wave coming toward him. The wave pushed him out of the deeper water and toward the shore. Spencer fought it, trying to get back to Justin. But the wave was too strong. It carried him all the way to the shallow section. He stood up, frantically looking around for Justin. Then he saw another wave pushing Justin toward him. Justin floated next to him, choking and coughing out water as he struggled to stand up. Spencer grabbed his shirt and held his head above the water, while pulling him toward the shore. When they got to where it was only a foot deep, they sat down in the water to rest.

"Are you okay?" Spencer asked after Justin stopped coughing out water and started to breath normally again.

"Yah," Justin finally said. "I couldn't get to the surface. It was hard to swim with my clothes on." He looked around. "Good thing that wave pushed me to the shore."

Spencer agreed, as he looked across the water. The wind was calm, and the surface was perfectly smooth, like glass. *Where did the waves come from?* Spencer wondered if the wind had heard his cries for help.

Spencer took his shoes off and threw them onto the sand.

"I'm going to get cleaned off. You okay if we hang here for a little while?"

"Sure," Justin responded. He removed his shirt and shoes and threw them over to the shore as well. Spencer walked into the water to see how far Justin could safely go.

"You can't go any farther than right here," Spencer told him.

Justin nodded as he pushed as much water as he could at Spencer, splashing him in the face. Spencer splashed him back. The boys played in the water until their arms and legs grew tired. Then they rested in the warm, shallow water.

Spencer looked at Justin, thinking about how he could have drowned earlier. He noticed that the rainbow colors were no longer in his hair or on his face. He looked down at his own shirt and shorts and saw that they were back to their original colors. His shirt was white again. Spencer swam over and grabbed their shoes and Justin's shirt and splashed them around in the water until all the rainbow colors were gone. Justin's shoes returned to the bright white that they were when they were new.

# CHAPTER 10

After a while, they got out of the water to lie on the warm rocks. The sun started drying their clothes. After they got their shoes on and stood up, the wind circled around them until they were completely dry.

"We should be getting back," Spencer said to Justin. He wasn't sure how long they had been there. "We need to find the door."

The boys started walking toward the field of tall green grass and purple and yellow wildflowers.

"The door!" Justin yelled, "I see it!"

Spencer looked up and saw the semi-circle rainbow door standing in the field. They raced through the tall grass. Before touching the door, Spencer looked back at the colorful meadow and the big lake. He looked across the field to where the rainbow used to be. He reached up to touch his pendant and remembered with a pang of sadness that it was lost. He realized he should have made a wish on the giant rainbow to find it.

He turned back to the rainbow door and placed his palm in the middle of the door. Justin placed his hand next to Spencer's, and the door lifted up to let them back into the circular room of doors. The boys watched the door close behind them.

Spencer turned around to look at the giant blue marble in the center of the room. It seemed to glow more brightly as he looked at it, as if beckoning him to come over. He knew they had to get back to their house, but he couldn't leave without spending a few minutes at the marble structure. He walked to the center of the room, mesmerized by the beautiful blue glow. Since the last time they were there, he hadn't stopped thinking about that marble. It was perfectly round and about a foot taller than him. He looked at the wispy white cloud formations that stood out against the bright blue. He reached out and felt the cool, smooth surface. He slowly walked around the marble, dragging his fingertips along the surface. He stopped to stare at the white streak that was left where he had dragged his fingers. It reminded him of the white stripe that plane engines make in a clear blue sky. He watched as the stripe slowly disappeared. He took his hand down and continued to slowly circle the marble.

He bent down to look for the word "together" that they had seen the first trip, but the word wasn't there. He stood back up, planning to walk away, but the wispy clouds seemed to reach out to him, asking him to stay. He looked at the top of the round structure, wanting to climb and sit on top like last time. He looked closer at the top of the marble. It looked like something was there. He reached his hand to feel around, and his hand hit something. And he knew what it was!

"Justin! My chain and pendant!"

Justin ran over to see.

"I just found it on top of the marble!" Spencer said excitedly. "I can't believe it! I got it back!" He looked at the round silver pendant that was attached to a black braided leather chain. He looked at the crescent moon and stars on one side and flipped it over to see the infinity symbol on the other side.

"How'd it get from the square room to here?" Justin asked, pointing from the wall to the marble.

"I don't know," Spencer responded. "We didn't go near the marble after we left the square room. Remember? We went directly to the hallway door after we got back."

Justin nodded. "So, someone put it there."

Spencer felt the chills on his arms. "That means someone or something else is down here."

"Well, it's cool you got it back," Justin said.

Spencer stared at the pendant, deep in thought. *How did my necklace get here?* Finally, he put the chain around his neck and looked at Justin. "We better get back. We've been gone a long time. Lori is going to be so mad at us!"

"Maybe she won't know that we were gone — like last time," Justin suggested.

"I hope you're right. But I think we've been gone even longer this time."

They rushed over to the giant hallway door and placed their left hands on the big metal handle. Spencer was relieved when the door slowly opened a few feet to let them pass through. He heard the big door close as he followed Justin down the cold hallway to the big metal slide.

"I hope the return trip works like last time," Spencer said, feeling a little anxious about getting back. Justin sat on the edge of the slide with a silly grin on his face. Spencer knew Justin was looking forward to what was coming. Justin's eyes grew big as his hair stood up straight and his shirt started to lift. Spencer heard a *whoosh* as Justin started to slide backward *up* the slide. He watched Justin fly around the turns and disappear at the second curve. He couldn't see past that in the dark, but he could hear his brother's laughter as he flew the rest of the way up the slide.

Spencer realized that he had been holding his breath, and he let out a sigh of relief. He was happy it worked like last time. He sat down on the edge of the slide, eager to get out of the cold hallway. He felt his hair stand up and then the pull. He flew backward up the slide and around the curves. He slid up as fast and easily as he had slid down it. Then he slowed as he approached the top and was pushed off the slide and back under the couch.

"We need to go find Lori," Spencer said as soon as he crawled out from under the couch. He looked again at Justin's hair and clothes. Then he looked down at his white shirt and gray shorts. Their clothes looked dry and clean. There were no traces from the rainbow. "Let me do the talking. Remember, you can't tell anyone about the couch," Spencer said, looking Justin directly in the eyes. "Got it?"

"I know!" Justin said.

Spencer turned and headed for the family room. He was trying to make up a story to tell Lori. *Has she been looking for us? Is she going to be mad? What am I going to tell her?*

He jogged into the family room, nearly tripping over her big purse that was on the floor. Lori glanced over at them. "I'm so sorry, Lori," Spencer blurted out.

"What did you do?" Lori asked, narrowing her tired eyes at him. She looked over at Justin. "Anyone bleeding? Anything broken?"

He looked at the TV. Her show was still on. He turned and looked at the kitchen clock.

Again, according to the clock, they were only gone a short time. *How is that possible?* It felt like they had been gone a long time. He let out a huge sigh. Like the first time, what seemed like hours in the under-the-couch world was only minutes.

Lori was staring at him, waiting for a response. "Why are you sorry?" she repeated. "What did you do?"

"Um, well, it's more what we didn't do," Spencer stammered, trying to think quickly. "We didn't read like I said we would." It was the truth, and he was proud of his answer. He was glad he hadn't said more before he realized that they weren't in trouble.

"You still have time," she said, looking at him strangely. She glanced over at Justin. "Why did you run in here?"

"We want to watch the rest of the show, if I haven't missed too much," Spencer said quickly. Again, he was proud of his answer because it was the truth — he wanted to hear about the space aliens. Spencer was happy that he and Justin got to go on the adventure, he was able to get his pendant back, and now he got to watch the show. He loved anything about space. "Then maybe I can understand Justin a little better since he's an alien." Spencer smirked and pointed at Justin.

"No, I'm not! You're the one whose head is always in space! Maybe you're the alien!" Justin yelled back.

Lori sighed. "I think you both might be aliens."

"Really?" Justin asked with big eyes.

"No," she smiled. "Sit down and let's watch the show."

"But I'm hungry!" Justin said.

"Again?" Lori asked in her cheery voice. "You must be growing. Go grab a snack and then let's learn about aliens and spaceships. After the show, you two can get your reading done and then we'll start dinner for your mom."

# CHAPTER
# 11

Their mom got home late from work and was happy to find that Lori had prepared dinner before she left. Justin told her about how he helped to mash the potatoes. Spencer could see that she looked tired. He set the table without being asked.

While his parents talked about work at dinner, Spencer focused on his plate. He couldn't stop thinking about the day. He was only half-listening as his dad talked about his business trip, and his mom talked about her meetings. Finally, they stopped talking, and his mother looked at Justin.

"Did you guys get to the library today?"

Justin nodded.

"Did you get some books that you'd like to read?" she asked.

Justin nodded again.

"I'd like to hear about what you read today. I assume you read like I asked you to this morning?" Spencer could hear the doubting tone in her voice. Justin quickly shoved a huge glob of mashed potatoes into his mouth and motioned for her to wait while he chewed. Spencer stifled a laugh. She didn't like them to talk with their mouths full of food, and he was using that rule to his advantage. Spencer looked at his mom's face. She had the "concerned mom" look on her face.

"It's important that you keep trying. The more you read, the easier it will get. It just takes practice. Now, tell me what you learned today."

Spencer stopped chewing and watched Justin. He knew that Justin was excited after their adventure and couldn't settle down to read. He watched as Justin chewed his potatoes slowly. He could tell he was thinking about how to answer her question. Finally, Justin swallowed his food and looked up at his mother.

"Today, I learned about rainbows," Justin said. Spencer whipped his head around to look at his brother. He was worried that Justin was going to tell her about their adventure.

"You read about rainbows?" his mother asked in a higher voice than normal.

Justin continued, not directly answering her question. "I learned there are seven colors in a rainbow. ROY-G-BIV is the *anocrim* for the colors."

"Do you mean *acronym*?" his mother asked, smiling.

"Yah," Justin answered. Then he proceeded

to list the colors of the rainbow from memory. Spencer knew it was easy for him to remember since he had not only gone through each color of the rainbow, but he had also *tasted* them. Justin proudly continued. "And the last two colors are indigo and violet. They both look purple, but they are different colors." Spencer couldn't believe how confident Justin sounded. He continued. "And did you know that rainbows happen after it rains and when the sun's rays go through the water in the sky?"

"That's right!" their dad said, nodding. "Did you know that two people can stand near each other and look at the same rainbow and see it differently? No two people see a rainbow exactly the same."

"Well, did you know that a rainbow happens when it's raining in one part of the sky and sunny in the other?" Justin asked back. Spencer stared at his brother in disbelief. He couldn't believe Justin was pulling this off. He looked at his parents and could see they were fully engaged in the conversation.

Justin hadn't read that day, but he had learned something from their adventure. And Spencer realized that his brother *had* been listening to him when he explained about the rainbow. At the time, Spencer thought he wasn't paying attention. Spencer looked over at his dad and could tell that he was enjoying the back-and-forth with Justin.

"Did you know that we only see a semi-circle from the ground, but if we looked at the same rainbow from an airplane, we would see a circle?" their dad asked.

"I didn't know that!" their mother said.

"Well, did you know you can actually taste the colors of a rainbow?" Justin asked. Spencer swung his head to look at Justin. *What is he doing?* Spencer kicked Justin's leg under the table to tell him to stop.

Their dad laughed. "I used to think that too! I imagined that the red was cherry, and the yellow was a tart lemon."

"Nope, it's pineapple," Justin replied. "And the green is sour apple."

"Not lime?" their dad asked, surprised. Spencer caught Justin's eyes and made a motion with his hand to tell him to be quiet. Fortunately, their dad thought Justin was playing.

Their mother seemed satisfied with Justin's response and turned to Spencer. "What did you read about today? Did you learn anything exciting like Justin did?"

Spencer felt his face get hot. The truth was that he didn't read either. He had planned to read, but like Justin, he was too excited and couldn't focus on his book. He looked at his mother and saw that she was waiting for his answer. He knew he couldn't pull off shoving a bunch of mashed potatoes in his mouth to stall for time like his brother had. But as he thought about it, like Justin, he had learned something on their adventure. He wasn't sure he could explain it but tried to put his thoughts into words.

"I learned that sometimes you can't control things, no matter how hard you try.

Sometimes, you have to let go," Spencer said, remembering Justin yelling at him to let go when he was trying to keep him from flying away. Spencer thought about the wind whispering to him to let go and go with the flow. He looked up and saw that both of his parents were intently listening to him.

"Wow," his mother said. Spencer could tell that she was surprised by what he said. "Say more so I better understand what you mean."

Seeing that his parents were interested in what he said made him feel more confident. "Sometimes, you need to go with the flow and let the wind take you where it will." *And you will not be disappointed*, he thought to himself. He smiled as he remembered the incredible feeling of flying with the wind. He looked up. His parents were staring at him with strange looks on their faces. Finally, his father spoke.

"That was deep. But I think I get what you mean. It's like when we went rafting in the mountains last summer. Remember how our guide joked with us that we had to paddle upstream? It's nearly impossible. We knew we couldn't fight the river's current. Instead, we dropped the oars, so to speak, and let the flow of the river take us downstream."

"The path of least resistance," his mother added.

Spencer watched as his parents talked about "letting go." He looked over at Justin, who had a confused look on his face. He knew Justin had no idea what they were talking about. Spencer smiled and winked. Justin reached across the table for more potatoes and gravy as his parents continued to talk.

# CHAPTER
# 12

Later that night, as they were getting ready for bed, Spencer walked into Justin's room. "Hey, that was great at dinner. I can't believe you remembered what I told you about the rainbows. I honestly didn't think you were listening."

Justin shrugged his shoulders. "Sometimes I'm listening, even when it looks like I'm not," he explained. "Especially when I like the topic."

Spencer looked at his brother. That made total sense to him. He felt the same way when he read a book. He enjoyed reading topics that interested him but struggled to read something he found boring.

Justin smiled and jumped up and down. "Today was awesome. We got to fly, and we got to touch and taste the rainbow. I wish we could do that every day!"

"Me too," Spencer responded. He had promised himself that he would only go back one time, just to get his pendant back. But he had so much fun that he wanted to go back again.

"I wish we could go to the same place tomorrow," Justin said.

"I wonder if the rainbow door will be there the next time we go," Spencer answered. "I hope it doesn't disappear like the square door did."

"No, it can't! I want to fly through the rainbow again," Justin said.

Spencer nodded. "I've always dreamed about flying."

They talked for a while longer about the different flavors of the rainbow and how they loved flying through the air. Spencer laughed, recalling what Justin looked like covered in all those rainbow colors. He looked at his colorful shirt and saw that he had a glob of gravy on the front but no stains from the rainbow.

As Spencer lay back on his pillow, he gazed at the glow-in-the-dark stars and moon on his ceiling and thought about the day. He wondered again how the four moons on the ceiling in the circular room had changed from being full moons to waning gibbous moons. He didn't understand why he didn't recognize any of the star formations. He wondered if whoever created the ceiling didn't think about the formations. Or maybe it wasn't from his solar system.

Deep in thought, he reached up and touched his pendant. He was really glad to have it back but got chills thinking about how it got on top of the marble. He thought about the green eye that he saw in the wall, and about the knock and reflection. *Is something down there? Did it find my chain?* He knew he would get nightmares if he fell asleep thinking about the eye and the reflection. He made himself think about happier things.

Spencer could still see Justin flying in circles in the sky, smiling from ear to ear. He was enjoying himself while Spencer was fighting with the wind to stay on the ground. He could hear the voice whispering in his ear to "let go." He thought about being tossed through the different layers of the rainbow and tasting every color. He shuddered as he remembered the frantic moments in the lake when Justin was drowning.

The adventure was so much fun and such an incredible experience, but it reminded him that they had to be careful. There was real danger in the under-the-couch world. He thought he was going to die in the cube on the first adventure, and now Justin had a close call in the lake on this second trip. But both times they managed to get home safely and without Lori knowing that they were gone.

He had to admit that he had an amazing day. He had so much fun with Justin. He still thought his brother was annoying but was grateful that Justin was with him today. He made all the fun happen.

Spencer recalled how much he had missed his friends earlier that day. But today ended up being one of the best days ever. He closed his eyes, smiling, looking forward to going back under the couch for another adventure.

SUSAN LINTONSMITH went from climbing the corporate ladder to falling under the couch.

Susan is the author of the Under the Couch chapter books, *Hide and Seek*, *Rainbow*, and *Spiders*.

She has lived in Colorado for most of her life and loves sports, the mountains, and spending time with her family and two dogs. With the support of her husband and sons, she took a break from her thirty-year business career to follow her dream and write books based on the stories she told her two sons when they were young.

Her goal is that all kids, especially those who struggle with reading like her boys, will enjoy the adventures Spencer and Justin go on in the Under the Couch series.

Visit her website at underthecouchbooks.com.

Look for other books in the Under the Couch series, including book one, *Hide and Seek*, and book three, *Spiders*.

Made in the USA
Columbia, SC
27 January 2022

54910150R00064